Randolph C. Nyce is of Indigenous descent of the Haisla band or tribe. He is one of the chiefs of the Beaver Clan. Chief GWASACHS. He was born on March 16th, 1949.

This book is dedicated to my mother, Laura Williams, who has always been my biggest supporter.

Randolph C. Nyce

THE WITCH AND THE WISEMAN

AUSTIN MACAULEY PUBLISHERS™
LONDON • CAMBRIDGE • NEW YORK • SHARJAH

Ordering Information
Quantity sales: Special discounts are available on quantity purchases by corporations, associations, and others. For details, contact the publisher at the address below.

Publisher's Cataloging-in-Publication data
Nyce, Randolph C.
The Witch and The Wiseman

ISBN 9798891552265 (Paperback)
ISBN 9798891552272 (ePub e-book)

Library of Congress Control Number: 2024904880

www.austinmacauley.com/us

First Published 2024
Austin Macauley Publishers LLC
40 Wall Street, 33rd Floor, Suite 3302
New York, NY 10005
USA

mail-usa@austinmacauley.com
+1 (646) 5125767

Table of Contents

Chapter 1
Day of Darkness

This day was looking promising of warmth and sunshine. It had already been a very good summer for us, and it was only mid-July, with a couple of summer months still to come.

As usual, my children Karen and William had slept late and were just now coming downstairs for breakfast. My daughter Karen had just turned twelve over a month ago; she had been born in June of 1934. My son William, a couple of years younger than Karen, was ten years old. Unfortunately, they had lost their mother to tuberculosis a few years ago. So, the last few years have been especially trying for both my children, but it really showed how resilient children can be.

As we sat eating our breakfast, we discussed what the plans were for that day, and it was no surprise to me that their plans were to go swimming in the ocean at high tide. The children liked to swim in an area that we called "The Bay". The reason that they liked to swim there was because of the outcropping of rock that protruded out into the ocean and protected The Bay from the prevailing south winds. No matter how rough the ocean got, it was always calm in the bay. The bay was at the south end of our village, and it was distanced from the main village. The only way to get there was through a narrow trail about three-quarters a mile from the main village.

So, about 2 p.m. that afternoon, I gave my children a hug and instructed them to be careful as they left for the bay. The reason that I had asked them to be careful is that the more adventurous of the children liked to swim in an area they named The Octopus Bed. Why they had named it that, I don't know. However, the Octopus Bed was not protected by the outcropping of rock and was open to the wind and rough waves. I know the reason for doing this because, believe it or not, I was a child once and had liked swimming in the waves.

The rest of the day for me I spent puttering around the house, tending to whatever needed to be done. I had a large pile of my winter's supply of firewood; every once in a while, I would split a few blocks and pile it in my woodshed. Although it was too warm to start my wood stove, we would need water to be heated so my children could bathe in our old galvanized tub. We didn't have the luxury of having fresh water for both of them, so they would have to take turns and share the same water; I knew that they would both be home about six pm and would make sure that dinner was cooked by then, and we could let the stove go out.

As per our usual routine, my children arrived home at about six p.m. and had their baths; then, we sat down for dinner. This was my favorite time of day; as we had our dinner, my children were talking over each other, excitedly talking about the events of the day.

After dinner, my usual routine, which I did that day, was to grab a coffee and sit in my front yard to unwind from the day. My front yard was on the east side of the house, in the shade from the sun, at almost nine p.m. I was getting things ready for the night, making sure we had water for the morning. Satisfied everything was in place for tomorrow. I was just about to sit down and relax when I heard what all Haisla's dreaded. Three shots had rang out, what was a signal that we all knew was a call for help. Whenever this happened, we all knew to meet at the church. I made it there as quickly as possible. When I got there, about forty or fifty people had gathered there already. I could see that a young mother was obviously in distress and crying, with her husband consoling her. I learned that their two young daughters had not returned from their swimming trip that day. The parents had already searched the bay to no avail. With darkness looming, a quick plan was put together. Three people who had boats would search the shoreline, and four groups of men would search the forest around Cimocha.

As was expected, we didn't really have time to do a good search before darkness set in. Everyone gathered in front of the church to make arrangements for daybreak. At first light, we all departed in prearranged groups; we would do a grid search in the forests surrounding our village. There were six groups of men doing this search; there were four boats crisscrossing the ocean in front of our village. They used all different types of contraptions to which large fishing hooks were attached and would be used to drag the ocean floor.

After a long, tiring, fruitless day, everyone met again in front of the church. It was there that we learned that the two young sisters were ages nine and eleven. It was decided that the next day would be a repeat of today but that the groups searching the forest would expand the distances of their search grids.

This went on for five days when it was concluded that, unfortunately, the young girls were lost forever. The men searching the forest were all accomplished hunters and knew what to look for; not one clue, not the one track or footprint, was seen by anyone. Family and a few friends continued to search for weeks, but even they finally accepted that it was futile and gave up the search.

Chapter 2
Ubah-Dee

My grandfather, whose English name was James Clarkson, but our whole family affectionately called him Ubahdee; actually, I don't recall any Haisla ever calling him by his English name. Everyone called him Ubah Dee. In that era, when he was born, there were no birth certificates, but we believed him to be about eighty-five years old. He suffered from some affliction to his eyes that rendered him almost completely blind. It was uncertain how blind, probably eighty-five to ninety percent blind(ness). He could only see in shadows. Being a hard worker all his life stood him in good stead at this stage of his life. He was a tough old man; he lived on a hill above the shoreline, and we would all help him get firewood for the winter. We would tow in driftwood logs to the beach below his house, cut it up, and pack the blocks up to his house. He insisted on splitting and piling the wood himself. It would scare me to watch him split the wood. He would use his hands and feel the top of the block before each swing of the axe. I was always afraid that he might miss and injure himself, but his aim was always true. Many times, family members would ask him to live with someone in one of our families, but he would always refuse.

He was fiercely independent. He was a great storyteller, and I could sit and listen for hours of his hunting and fishing exploits as a young man. He had what I call a silent laugh; the corner of his eyes would crinkle, and his shoulders would bob up and down; that was the only way I could tell he was laughing.

Ubah dee had no formal education whatsoever but was one of the most intelligent people I have ever known. Unbeknownst to us, he possessed powers that we would witness later on in his life.

So this was my grandfather, a man who our whole family cherished and loved. I have no doubt that he would lay down his life for any one of his family; he loved us all that much.

Chapter 3
Re-Visited

Summer was pretty much over, although we still experienced fairly warm days. This being mid-September, the children had been back to school for almost two weeks. Our old two-classroom school sat atop a hill overlooking our village. I can't fathom the difficulty that the two teachers had. Firstly, they had to put up with being isolated from September to June. Secondly, they had to find a way to teach from grades one to six to students in two classrooms. They always seemed to find a way to do it.

The only way into our village was by boat. Any teachers that came here would have to make their way to Victoria, B. C. They would then take the supply ship that came here every seven to eight weeks. We had two small stores here; one was called Sunrise, and the other was simply called "supply". The store supply had a limited amount of clothing, rain gear, boots and jackets, and also canned foods. Sunrise had mostly foodstuff, mostly canned.

This is why there was a need for the supply ship. Also, the school had a coal furnace, and the ship would bring tons of coal at least twice a year.

We had one wharf, which had one float attached to it. The float was about seventy feet long and eight feet wide. The wharf jutted out about one hundred feet into the ocean. The wharf was about ten feet wide, and at the end of it, it widened to about sixty feet wide; this is where the supply ship would be moored.

This day in mid-September was so peaceful and quiet that it seemed like there was nothing that could disturb this peace, that is, until the dreaded signal for distress rang out. At approximately 5 p.m., three shots rand out, and as per normal procedure, everyone made their way to the church. Harry, the chief councilor, was the spokesman there. He told us two of the children had stayed at school for extra help and had not made it home. Of course, all of their friend's homes had been contacted in case they had stopped off there. No one had seen either one, a boy and a girl, both nine years old and in the same class.

It was decided that search parties would be arranged as soon as possible but that the search would not proceed until the next day. The reason was that at this time of year, it got dark much earlier, and any sign of what may have happened would be trampled on. This time, however, it was decided that this would be an expanded search. All groups were arranged and were instructed to bring enough food and water at t least two days. All were to meet on the hill coming down from the school at first light. All were told, DO NOT start the search until everyone was there!

The next morning, at first light, all search parties were gathered outside the school. The road coming down from the school had a plateau above it. On this plateau, there was the mostly deciduous tree, Alder, and there were a few

Evergreens, Hemlock and Balsam. This was the most obvious place to start the search. It was decided only four of our best hunters/trackers would go in here to lessen the chance of disrupting any clues. They weren't in there very long, and when they were done, everyone met at the church. Of the four people that went into the plateau, my brother Rick was the spokesman. He said, this is what we found; we couldn't find any tracks leading in. What we did find is that a person sat underneath the Hemlock tree, watching the road. It appears that this person is small in stature, possibly a woman.

Now it appears that when this person took the two children, one was left. On the ground, while the other was taken away. It's difficult to say, based on what we had seen, if the child left there was bound with a roll or not. Why didn't this child just walk away? Also, there was no sign of tracks leading away.

It was decided that two search parties would scour the hills and mountains to the south of the village. The other three parties would look north and northeast of the village. Each party consisted of five men, all armed and with provisions. For at least two days, the plan was for them all to return on the third day. Now, for the rest of the people, it was a time for waiting and praying.

At troubled times like this, the rest of the village would all pull together. The women of the community had meetings to decide who would cook for the two families for the next few days. It was not only the sharing of food, but the companionship meant a lot to people who were going through difficult times.

At around eleven in the morning, the first group of searchers returned home.

First, it was plain to see that they were all very tired and relieved to be home. The remaining four groups would surely be as tired as this group was. They had all traveled some of the most rugged terrain possible. Also, some of the groups traveled and covered more distance than their fellow searchers.

It was decided that we would wait till the last group arrived to have a meeting at the church. In the meantime, almost all families prepared something for a potluck at the church.

At around 5:30 p.m., the last group arrived and were directed to the church. Around 6:30 p.m., everyone had been fed, and each group talked to the community about their findings.

Only the group that had traveled the furthest Northeast of the village had come across possible clues. They were within sight of possibly the highest mountain in this area. The Haisla had yet to give this mountain a name.

It was an opening in the forest where they thought there might be a clue. They said because of the mossy forest floor, it was difficult to really see tracks. They said what they had seen was a possible indent on the moss where a child could possibly have lain.

It was decided that this wasn't enough to warrant an all-out search of this area. As the old saying goes, "Hindsight is 20/20". We didn't realize it then, but this group was very close!!!

Chapter 4
The Hunt

Even with all the turmoil that the Haislas were undergoing, the tragedies with the loss of a lot of our children, life had to go on; Plans & preparations had to be made for this coming winter. Therefore, an extended moose hunt was being planned for the Dala & Kildala rivers.

It was decided that we would leave in two days, so preparations got underway, with food, bedding, and clothing being packed, enough for a stay of up to a week and a half.

On the day we were to leave, the elders decided that we would leave at midnight in order to get to the delta of the Kildala River at high tide. We were blessed with clear skies and a full moon that night as we left.

The canoes that we used, which were built by my grandfather, were about 45ft long and 4ft wide, very seaworthy craft. Each canoe easily accommodated all of our belongings and seven people in each canoe. The bowmen in each canoe were the ones who set the pace. The Helmsman steered the canoe; in this case, my grandfather was the Helmsman in one canoe, and my grandmother was the

Helmsman in the other canoe, which was most unusual. I've never heard of a woman being a helmsman for a canoe.

As we departed, our enthusiasm had to be curbed by our grandfather. He spoke out loud to our two bowmen, my brother Rick and my uncle Les. He told them to set a long-distance pace, saying that if we kept up this pace, we'd be burnt out long before we reached our destination.

On this night, we were blessed with clear skies and a full moon. We were heading into a strong South wind with waves about 3' high. I'd have to say we must have made an impressive sight with 12 paddles flashing in the moonlight. This wasn't the only thing flashing in the moonlight. The two canoes, traveling about 20' apart, would ride up the crest of the waves and come crashing down into the trough. Each time the canoes would come down into the trough, these would send plumes of water away from the Bow. The water droplets glistened like millions of diamonds in the moonlight.

After about two hours of traveling south on the Douglas Channel, we turned East into the Kildala Arm. As we entered the Kildala Arm, we lost two things. We no longer had moonlight as the moon disappeared behind the mountains to the West of us.

And we no longer had the wind to contend with, as Kildala Arm was protected from the wind by the mountains on both sides of the channel.

My grandfather yelled out and motioned for the canoes to come together, and within minutes, the canoes were lashed together. He said it was time to rest and eat; we'll let the tide work for us. Sure enough, we were being pushed at a speed of about 3 knots towards our destination. Within minutes, the gas stoves had heated tea for us, which we had with ready-made sandwiches; our grandfather took this time to give us last-minute instructions. He said, when we get close to Atkins Bay and Dala River, listen for my whistle. When you hear it, I want you to go into the silent mode. There was a way to paddle where it was almost impossible to hear the paddles enter and be withdrawn from the water.

About an hour and a half later, we heard my grandfather's signal. Everything was going as planned until my daughter Karen accidentally hit the side of the canoe with her paddle. On a calm night like tonight, the sound carried a great distance! We could all feel how badly Karen felt, and we sympathized with her. My grandfather lightened the moment by yelling out very loudly, "Good morning!" This indicated to us there was no longer any need to be silent.

The skies to the East of us were starting to brighten as we neared the Delta of the Kildala River. It was just as my grandfather planned; we were able to paddle a good portion of the river. It was only in the last twenty minutes, as we neared the camp that we had to use the poles to move the canoes.

The first few hours after reaching camp were spent cleaning out the cabins and getting heat into the cabins to rid them of dampness. Once this was done, I called my children Karen, who was 12, and William, who was 10. We went to the woodshed, where we each grabbed a block of wood and carried it to the river bank to be used as our chairs. The only thing missing now were drinks, which we went to get: coffee for me and hot chocolate for my children.

As we sat down to discuss plans for tomorrow, our senses went into overdrive, taking in all our surroundings. The sounds, the smells, the sights. I could smell the wet leaves, pine needles, and Cedar trees. The fall colors of Alder and cottonwood leaves. The yellows, reds, and orange colors. It was almost as if a master artist had done all this. Come to think of it, a master artist had done all this. The thing that topped it all off was the gentle sound of the river flowing by.

The aura of all this, I think, mesmerized all three of us. My children become unusually quiet. In the next short while, I went over the silent signals that I would use tomorrow to instruct my children when it came time to hunt.

Conventionally, everyone had always gone for a heart or lung shot, which was good, but a lot of meat was wasted this way. In our target practices, I told my children that we would be no further than 70 yards away and to go for a head or neck shot. My children had become very proficient at shooting targets at 70 yards with their 30-30 rifles. I felt they were ready for this hunt, where I hoped they would get their first moose.

The next morning, everyone was busy getting the canoes loaded. Three of my brothers, Rick, Bo, and Keith, would be going downriver to hunt the Dala River and Atkins Bay. My uncles Les, Bill, and Scotty would be going upriver about two miles. After breakfast, both canoes departed for their destinations. Since it was not quite daylight, we would wait awhile before we crossed the river.

As we crossed the river, I couldn't help but notice how excited my children were.

We tied up the rowboat and started our hike to an area that I had hunted many times. Since we were also in grizzly bear country, I instructed my children to have a bullet in the chamber and to be sure that the safeties were on. We arrived at the site where I hoped we would be able to call a moose in. It was an area that had a lot of willow bark, and a good sign was that a lot of willow bark had been stripped clean, which was what moose fed on. We walked about fifty feet up a small hill to a spot that overlooked this whole area of willows. My children sat about two feet below me. When we were settled in and comfortable, I gave my first moose cow call. I had instructed my children that when using the calling method, they had to be prepared to sit for one or two hours and not to call no more than three or four times.

I had called twice in the forty-five minutes that we were there when I caught movement to my right about seventy yards out. I tapped both my children on their shoulders and pointed to where I saw movement. About five minutes later, we all saw a bull moose as it was moving slowly to where it had heard my calls. Now, it was time to use our per-arranged signals. I squeezed both my children's arms, which meant getting ready. The moose kept inching closer to where we were until it was about fifty yards away. I tapped both my children on the shoulders to bring up their guns. The moose was now standing broadside to us, and I used my forefingers to instruct them to aim. When they were both aiming for a few seconds, I tapped them both on the head. BOOM! Both shots rang out. as one, and the moose was down. We quickly made our way to where the moose lay. There is an old Haisla Tradition that we must pay respect to an animal that has given up its life so that we may survive. My children did this by patting the moose on its side and saying, "nolok", nolok, nolok. When they were done, I checked for where this animal was hit. I didn't know if my children had discussed this, but one shot to the head and one shot to the neck, this moose had not suffered. As I told my children, this was grizzly country, and we had to clean and quarter this animal very fast! So, in fifteen minutes, the job was done. I put two front quarters into my pack board and a hind quarter each into my children's pack boards. I cut two handholds into the rib cage's fur side down. Again, while making it to the river, we made sure to have one bullet in the chamber.

I took the rib cages and packs of moose across the river before picking up the children. We hung the moose quarters in one smoke shed and the rib cages in another shed. The rib cages would be smoked together with what my uncles and brothers would bring.

My brothers and uncles had brought enough provisions for two days, so we probably wouldn't see them till tomorrow afternoon. In the meantime, my children, still excited from their first hunt, were telling everyone for about the third time how they had bagged their first moose. I didn't say a thing, but I was proud of how they had handled themselves.

The next day, we all awoke with great anticipation. Had the rest of our crew been successful? Had they got their quota of moose? That question was partially answered at about noon. We heard my brothers long before we saw them. The whooping and hollering told us that they had been successful. Sure enough, when they arrived, they had two moose aboard, all cleaned and quartered. In short order, we had all the meat hanging in the two sheds.

At about three p.m., my uncles arrived very quietly; we didn't know they were there until their canoe was being tied up. They had also been successful with two moose all ready for the sheds.

After two days of hanging, the work began. Most of the meat would be canned, and some of it salted. The ribs would be smoked for about six hours, which we would dine on for dinner before we started on our journey home.

On the third day, all the canning and salting had been completed, and the canoes were loaded for our journey home.

As we made our way downriver, I could only say one thing: the mood of our crew was very happy! Our winter's supply of meat had been taken care of. It was a happy journey home!!!

Chapter 5
People of The Snow

The Haisla were known as "People of The Snow" and were aptly named! This was mid-January, and overnight, we had probably about four feet of snow. The kind of winter we were having, the amount of snow and cold we had already had, we wrongly thought we were safe from what was happening to our children. We were so mistaken. Everyone had just begun digging our way out when we heard someone yelling for help. The sound wasn't too far off, so I ran through the snow towards where I heard the calls for help came from. When I got to the house that needed help, there were already a number of people there. The frantic parents were telling everyone there that their son was missing! When the parents calmed down somewhat, a couple of men went into their home with them. When checking the boy's bedroom, it was found that the bedroom window was slightly ajar. On further study, it was seen that the snow below the window had been disturbed. To the dismay of the parents, it was decided that it would do no good to mount a search. There were no tracks leading to or away from the house. Also, the snow was so deep around the village and surrounding forest that it would be impossible to do any searching whatsoever. It seemed so harsh a decision to come to, but the Haisla had no other recourse than to abandon any thought of mounting a search.

A quick decision was made that after a pathway had been cleared all around the village, we would have a meeting at the church. The way we always did the snow clearing is that I would shovel about a three-foot wide path to the next house, and my neighbor would do the same. This went on until a pathway had been shoveled all the way to our wharf. Extra volunteers would shovel and clear our whole wharf. Also, extra help was needed to clear a pathway up to the school. There was never a shortage of volunteers for all this.

A few hours later, most of the community members met at the church. The reason for this meeting was not to discuss a search party because anyone could see that this was impossible.

There was a reason for optimism that the missing children were still alive. Almost every family in the village noticed that children's clothing was missing from their clotheslines, and food was also going missing. Knowing that they might still be alive and knowing how to find them was a perplexing question that haunted the Haisla.

It was decided at this meeting that an all-out search would again be launched as soon as the snow melted in the forest. The men decided that they were to be prepared to search for at least a week.

As was to be expected, this had turned out to be a very harsh winter. By the end of January, it was estimated that at least fourteen feet of snow had fallen on Haisla land.

For certain, a person had to be fairly tough to survive winters in this village. The people here had a certain grit about them. Most faced the onset of each winter in a stoical manner.

After all, we were The People of The Snow.

Chapter 6
Jux-Win

(Eulachon/Oolichan)

With another harsh winter behind them, the Haisla had what was almost a yearly ritual for them. The first or second week of March was usually an exciting time for the Haisla. They awaited the arrival of the oolichans or, as the Haisla call it, Juxwen. A small fish belonging to the smelt family was referenced by many names, known as candlefish or silverfish.

The first order of business for my family was to inspect our two canoes to make sure they were seaworthy. Next, the oolichan net was inspected to make sure that there were no tears in it. If any were found, it was patched immediately.

This was the fourth day of March, and the canoes were being loaded with needed equipment and food. The canoes sat on the beach and were all loaded as we waited for the tide to reach them. We estimated that the tide would reach the canoes around 11:00 a.m., and we would be ready with our personal belongings.

Finally, the time arrived, and we were underway. Our destination was the river with no name, four miles to the North of our village. There were ten family members on this trip, five in each canoe. From the time we left till we arrived at our camp, about three miles up the river, four and a half hours had elapsed.

With five people in each canoe, we had four people paddling and one Helmsman.

This made it a fairly relaxing trip.

Once we arrived at our camp, the two cabins were cleaned out, and the cots were set up. This was always a busy time, making sure everything was ready. The stoves in each cabin were lit to rid each cabin of any moisture.

The next day was a very busy time. We fell two hemlock and one cedar tree for our firewood. We spent all day bucking up these trees and packing them into our cabins.

The next day was spent splitting and piling all this wood.

Now that we had enough firewood, our attention was turned to getting the oolichan bins ready. The two bins were twenty feet by twenty feet and four feet high. The walls of these bins were constructed of cedar shakes. The bins were situated as close to the river as possible to make unloading the oolichans easier. Upon inspection, the bins only needed minor repairs from the previous season. We used the branches of the trees we had fallen to line the floor of the bins. This prevented the oolichans from coming into contact with the bare ground.

It was now a waiting game; we never had any idea how long the wait would be.

The important thing is that all preparations were made.

The oolichan nets we used were called, Ta-kaltha. These nets were almost funnel-shaped and were of various sizes, depending on who made them. The netting was very close together to prevent the oolichans from getting out. The large end of it was about five feet in diameter, and the back end was about eighteen inches in diameter. Now, we needed to cut posts that were eight to ten inches in diameter. These posts were driven into the river bed. The two posts were about five feet apart, the same distance as the diameter of the net mouth. Before setting the net, the back end of the net was tied closed to prevent oolichan from going straight through. A strip of wood was used to hold the mouth of the net open; otherwise, the net would collapse, and oolichans couldn't get in.

As the net filled, the hydraulic force of the river prevented the oolichans from swimming back out. When the net was full, the back end of the net would be pulled into the canoe. Once the back end of the net was aboard the canoe, the back end would be opened, and the oolichans drained into the canoe. We would continue to pull the net onto the canoe, working our way to the mouth of the net. This was done until the net was finally emptied, then re-set again.

In the early hours of the fifth morning, the sea lions announced the arrival of the oolichans. The sea lions were very loud animals. When they broke the surface, they would expel air almost violently and loudly from their lungs.

We had heard them before daylight, which caused everyone to excitedly throw whatever we had to have a very quick breakfast. The net would not take long whatsoever to set because everything was ready. As the skies began to brighten, we loaded the net onto the canoe and saw all the company we had. Sea lions and seals were busily chasing the oolichans and gorging themselves. Hundreds of seagulls were diving for oolichans, also gorging themselves. About twenty to twenty-five eagles were also feeding. This was an exciting and busy time for everyone. It appeared that this was the biggest oolichan run in many, many years! By around noon on the third day of fishing, both oolichan bins were full to the top. It was decided that we would smoke our oolichans here at the river; my son and my uncle Les would stay and tend the smokehouse and also fish for steelhead. So the next morning, only the three of us were in camp. Everyone else had gone back to the village for a couple of days.

The routine for the three of us was pretty much the same every day. We would start the fire in the smokehouse, then go check the salmon net for steelhead. .

We already had twelve steel heads in the smokehouse. On the second day, we sat on the rocky river bank, having tea, bread, and roasting oolichans over an open fire. These oolichans we were roasting were from last year. They had been smoked and were very well dried so that these could be kept for a long time. While we were eating, my son William said, 'Ubah-Dee said another child has been taken.' Les and I looked at my son and said when did Ubah0dee say this to you? he said, 'He told me just now,' I said, 'William, that's not possible; he's not here,' William said, 'Dad, we have been talking this way for a long time. Of course, Les and I were completely stunned by this. We didn't think mental telepathy was even possible. William said Uba-Dee says to tell you they will be here tomorrow to start getting wood for the boilers. For now, we had to wait and see before we knew whether to believe him or not. It took some time trying to digest what my son had told us. Disbelief is what I was feeling at the moment.'

The rest of our family arrived quite early, considering the distance they had come. We had already picked three cedar trees that we would use for the boiling of the oolichans to obtain their oil. It had to be a particular type of cedar. The way to tell if it was very dry cedar was to look at the very top. If the top was almost dead-looking with no nettles, it would be very dry.

The three trees had fallen and bucked up over the next two days. We transported it from the river banks upstream from our camp down to where we would be boiling the oolichans. When all this wood was split and piled close to the fire pits, the next job was to ready the two boilers and also get the fire pits prepared. The walls of the fire pits were concrete, about four inches thick. The walls of the boilers were hemlock slabs about three inches thick with sheet metal floor at the bottom.

The boilers were about five feet long by three feet wide and three feet high. The fire pits were purposely measured so that only the metal floor would be exposed to the flames. Before the boiling process started, we collected clay from the river banks. This would be spread rather thickly on top of the concrete to give some insulation at the bottom edges of the boilers.

Now, the boilers were all prepared and were ready for the rendering of the oolichan oil. The oolichans in the bins were left for four or five days to give them time to break down. If the boiling began too soon when the oolichans were still too fresh, the oil return would not be that much.

During all this hard work, the plight of the Haislas was always in the back of our minds. Although the loss of so many children was tragic, we could not abandon the necessities of life. Oolichan oil was the most valuable trading commodity of the Haisla. To this day! The oil was sought by villages up and down the coast.

On the fifth day, we started our boiling of oolichans with two boilers going. The boiling from start to finish normally took about four hours. To speed up the process, once the oolichans were boiling, specially constructed mashers were used to break up the oolichans. When it was felt that the maximum amount of oil could be had, the burning cedars were pulled out of the fire pit. Then, for all the spots that were still hot and boiling slightly, we would pour a small amount of cold water into them. This would continue until it was fairly cool and most of the oil had floated to the top. We would use specially constructed skimmers to skim the oil off, which we would put in metal pails. Once all the oil had been taken, we would lower red hot rocks into the pails of oil. This would purify the oil, and any bacteria would be burnt off.

The next step would be to pull the plugs on both boilers, and the sludge would drain into a chute and into the river. The boilers would then be refilled with water, and the whole process would begin again! For each boiler, when the water would start to boil, we would use galvanized tubs to carry the oolichans to put into the boilers.

Each tub was about three feet in diameter by two feet deep.

This whole process took about three days. Then, the cooled oil would be put into wooden barrels; each one would carry about thirty gallons. Since this was a banner year for the oolichan run, our family went home with nine barrels, which equated to two hundred and seventy gallons.

The pack home took two trips, which we did over two days. This had been a very successful season!

Chapter 7
The Witch

Now that we were back home and rested up from what had been a very good oolichan and oil-making trip, we were being filled in on what had transpired while we were away. The latest child that had been taken was an eleven-year-old boy. Apparently, this happened while he was on an errand packing water in from a nearby well.

What has been happening to the Haisla's has certainly changed their habits. It was always a known fact that the Haislas never locked their doors at night, and most people nailed their windows shut. All parents now walked their children to school and were there when school was out at the day's end.

Also, whoever or whatever was responsible for all this was becoming very bold. Apparently, every two or three nights, people were missing food from wherever they stored it, and clothing was being taken from clotheslines. Something had to be done.

A meeting was called for at the church, attended by the whole community. A plan was formulated that I thought might work. That day, everyone pitched in, gathering cedar, which was made into piles throughout the village. Seven large piles of cedar were placed strategically throughout the village.

All these piles of cedar were soaked with diesel. We were not certain of whoever or whatever we were laying a trap for could see at night. So we made certain that the three men at each pile were well camouflaged. All three men at each pile were armed with rifles, and the plan was if anyone saw anything that should not be there, let out a shrill whistle, and all piles would be immediately lit.

The first two nights were very quiet, with nothing amiss. The third night, however, was totally different. About halfway through the night, we were all startled to hear a shrill whistle from the northeast corner of our village. Poof! Poof! Poof! All seven piles of cedar were lit, turning our village to almost daylight! Within one minute after this happened, a shot rang out close to where we had first heard the whistle. Then, a loud commotion with all three men yelling in Haisla, saying here! Here! Come here! All the men left their stations and ran towards the sounds of voices. We all got to them about the same time, and all three men were visibly shaken. We asked them, what happened? The man that answered, Horace, said, 'I shot her! I shot her!' I asked, Who did you shoot? He said I think she was a witch because when I shot her, she was flying through the air!

Naturally, we were all dumbfounded by what he said. We asked have you guys been drinking? All three clarified what they had seen, and none of them had been drinking. Now we questioned Horace. Are you sure you shot her? We all knew Horace to be a good hunter and a good shot. He said, I also heard the bullet when it struck, and she didn't slow down! All hunters know that sometimes you can actually hear a bullet when it strikes home.

What we had witnessed tonight explained a lot. Some of the best trackers in this village could find no tracks or clues when trying to find this being because she left no tracks.

The next day, my grandfather UBah-Dee sent for me. I entered his house to the smell of coffee; he poured me a cup and said sit down, Son. He had heard what had transpired that night. The serious look on his face told me that we wanted to talk. He said, Son, the children are all alive; I can see them. I can see where they are being kept, but I don't know exactly where they are. So you must not allow this witch to be killed because if that happens, we may never find the children. They are in a shack inside what looks like a cave, and I see a lot of what looks like steam. Son, you have to let The People know what I've told you.

I knew UBah-Dee had special powers; what I did not know was that what he told me was just a small portion of the powers he possessed.

So I called a meeting of the whole community and passed on what UBah-Dee had told me. Of course, most of the people were skeptical of what I had told them but would honor what UBah-Dee had requested.

Even though a lot of the people were skeptical of what UBah-Dee had said, it changed the way they did things. The parents of the missing children in particular.

They would leave food out in cupboards on their porches, and children's clothes were also easily accessible. No one talked about this, but a lot of Haisla people took to doing all this also.

What was happening totally puzzled Haisla. The witch had to have known that it was totally wrong to be taking these children, but by the same token, she was looking after their well-being.

Even though the Haisla now knew that their children were still alive, they knew that they had to put a stop to the abduction of any more children! They also had to find a way to rescue their other children.

Chapter 8
Shelley

The Haisla People were all looking forward to the arrival of the supply ship, which was scheduled to be here the next morning. This ship came to our community about every seven to eight weeks. It would have goods to restock the shelves for our two small stores. Also, tomorrow, we will have tons of coal for the coal furnace of our school.

Even if the people weren't expecting anything, curiosity drove them to the dock when the ship arrived. This time was no different. I could sense the excitement of the people when the ship was sighted, still an hour out from the dockside.

When the ship was secured to the dock, the crewmen were very busy getting ready to unload all the goods and coal. Also, from one of the cabins, an R. C. M. P. officer emerged with two dogs. Apparently, the RCMP from Victoria had heard of the plight of the Haisla and sent this man to investigate. He walked up the ramp to the dockside with the two dogs. The big dog was on a tight leash and also had a muzzle on it.

The officer raised his hands to get the attention of The People and started to speak. He introduced himself as

Constable Shelley. He said he was of Scottish descent. He was a very big man, approximately six foot five inches, and about two hundred and sixty pounds. He also told the people not to get too close to the big dog, which he said was a purebred German Shepherd. He said, please do not attempt to pet it because it was a fighting dog. It, too, was like its owner, very big, weighing at least two hundred pounds. The smaller of the two dogs was a Hound of some sort, which he brought with him because of its tracking abilities.

He requested a place to bunk for the night. So I stepped forward. My grandfather's house was on a hill right above the dock, and he lived alone. I took Constable Shelley and introduced him to UBah-Dee, who welcomed him gladly.

After he got settled in, Constable Shelley wasted no time; he wanted to explore the village. He was very thorough; he walked the beach from one end of the village to the other end. He also spent hours walking the forest behind the village. When he was finished, he called for a quick meeting with the villagers. He said, if this being that has invaded your village could actually fly, it wouldn't matter where it entered the village.

Having said that, there are four possible entry/exit points that were identified for us.

While Constable Shelley had our attention, he laid out his plan. He let us know that they would need provisions for at least three days. He said that he would also need an ax with which to make himself a shelter each night.

At daybreak the next morning, we met with Constable Shelley as he prepared for his departure. His plan was to travel northeast from the village and search for any clues whatsoever of the missing children. He informed us that should he not return by the third day, we should look for him.

The afternoon of the third day arrived with no sign of Constable Shelley. A meeting was called, and it was decided that we should get ready to send out search parties the next day. There would be five groups of five armed men in each group.

At daybreak the next day, all five groups of searchers departed. The plan was for all five groups to travel parallel to each other; if the terrain allowed it, they would travel at least a half to three-quarter mile apart.

I was in the group at the center of all the groups, and we had been traveling now for about five hours when a shot rang out to the East of us. The terrain was fairly rugged, and we slowly made our way to the direction from which the shot had come. We had been traveling now for about half an hour when we could hear yelling voices.

We started yelling also, and we could hear men yelling over here. We finally reached two groups of searchers and could see from a distance that they were all upset.

Within a few minutes, we saw why they were upset. The scene that greeted us was the most horrific scene that I have ever witnessed; Constable Shelley and both dogs were deceased. That wasn't the worst part; all three had been beheaded! It was a scene that would haunt me for the rest of my life.

As we surveyed the scene, so many questions needed to be answered. Why didn't the constable use one of his firearms? We knew he had a rifle as well as a sidearm. Why had the big fighting dog not fought back at whatever caused this? And why wasn't it enough to just kill them all but to behead them also?

We decided to bury the dogs right there. We quickly made up a travois with which to transport Constable Shelley back to our village. By the time we were ready to begin our journey home, the last two groups of searchers had arrived.

It was almost nightfall by the time we arrived home. It was decided to leave the body of the constable at the church until morning.

The next morning, a cedar casket was constructed for the constable's burial. This man basically had given his life for the Haisla, and a full church service was warranted.

After the service and burial, UhBah-Dee sent for me. When we had found the bodies of the dogs and constable, no one put into words who or what had done the killing. Uh Bah-Dee, however, pulled no punches as he spoke. He said the reason the witch had beheaded all three is that was the only way to kill her was to also behead her; She thought everyone was the same. UhBah-Dee said we knew that shooting her wasn't the way to do it.

We know that something had to be done to find the children, and plans had to be made; this last tragedy was too much to ignore.

Chapter 9
The Message

After the tragic demise of Constable Shelley and his two dogs, it was decided that something had to be done. Plans had to be made, and the whole village gathered at the church. It was decided that an all-out effort had to be made to find the children. Six groups of men, five to a group, were chosen; each man was armed with a rifle and axe. We all carried backpacks with provisions for at least five days. It was felt that there was little chance that the children would be in the mountains to the South of the village, so only one group would search in that direction.

The next morning, we all left at daybreak. The group that I led would travel along the shoreline until we passed Minette Bay. The first six miles of our journey were through very rugged terrain and slow going. After about eight hours of travel, we finally reached the back end of Minette Bay. After a short climb, the countryside sort of flattened out and was much easier to travel. There was not much underbrush through the forest. The forest floor was covered in moss and was almost pleasant to walk on. About an hour later, we could hear voices to the East of Us, and we started yelling until they heard us. We joined up with this group and decided that we would have something to eat and bed down there for the night.

The next morning, after having coffee and moose jerky for breakfast, we continued on our journey. The group we had joined up with moved to the East of us again. We decided that today, we would travel about fifty feet apart but would always keep within sight of each other. These would increase our chances of spotting any type of clues that might have been left behind. About midday, our groups had a little excitement; we came within easy gunshot of a fairly large bull moose. This moose would have fed a lot of our people, but unfortunately, there was no time to be dealing with something like this.

We pushed on until about four o'clock in the afternoon when we came upon a rather large opening in the forest. From this vantage point, we could see a majestic mountain to the East of us. As of yet, this mountain, as far as we knew, had no name. There was not a cloud in the sky, but at the back part of this mountain, there were wisps of what appeared to be clouds. We decided to rest here and build a fire to cook our supper. After we had eaten, there were still hours of daylight left, so we decided to travel South for a while. If we continued in this direction, it would take us to the Eastern shore of the Douglas Channel. We decided after another two hours of traveling in this direction to make camp, and in the morning, we would decide in which direction we would travel.

The next morning, after a hearty breakfast, we decided that we would continue in a Northerly direction. Today, we would do what we had planned before we started this trip. We fired one shot into the air, and within about a minute, the group to the East of us also fired a shot. We were too far away to hear a shot from the group closest to them. The plan was if any group failed to fire an answering shot, the last group to fire a shot would then fire three shots, signifying that they needed help. We would then all travel towards the group that had fired three shots. Thankfully, in the days we were out there, this never happened. This day for our group proved to be uneventful. So, as the sun started to set, we made camp and readied for another night.

The next morning, as this was our third day, we decided that we would continue in a Northerly direction for a few hours, then turn back and start making our way home. Shortly after noon, we turned towards home. Making camp that evening was much easier; we used the same camp spot as the night before; therefore, no clearing of brush was needed. That night was the best night's sleep we all had. We had walked now many, many miles over some fairly rugged terrain.

After breakfast, we decided to alter our route slightly. We traveled East for about a half mile before continuing South. This way, we would be covering slightly different ground. No one said anything about how they were feeling, but I could read their faces. What I saw was a look of discouragement and fatigue. They were discouraged because we had found no clues whatsoever of the missing children.

Fatigue had also taken its toll on these Haisla men.

At the end of this fourth day, we were fairly close to the back of Minette Bay but would make camp now as it was close to sunset. Making camp in the dark was not an ideal situation.

While having breakfast on this, our last day in the forest, everyone seemed to be in good spirits, knowing that we would be home that night. We also decided that we would not travel too close to the shoreline as it was much too rugged.

We were still about two hours away from home when the sunset was built, and there would still be enough light to guide us home. As it turned out, we were the first group to make it home. My feeling was that the group that was farthest East might not make it home tonight. It turned out I was correct; only one other group made it home that night.

The next morning, the whole village waited anxiously for the remaining groups to arrive home. By one o'clock in the afternoon, the last remaining group had arrived, and it turned out that I was correct in guessing that the last group was the one that had traveled the furthest to the East.

As we had planned, everyone met at the church to discuss any findings of any of the groups. Nothing prepared us to hear what the groups that had traveled the furthest to the East. All the other groups had nothing to report.

The leader of this group called on a gentleman called George to relate to us all what had happened to him. George said he didn't know what time it was on their fourth night, only that it was the middle of the night when he was awakened by what he said was the witch. He sat there in the church telling us what happened. He said she awakened me by touching my face. I could see her face, and I could hear her talking to me, but her lips weren't moving. She had full control of my body; I could not make a sound if I wanted to. She said, get up, don't make any sound. She guided me a distance away from the camp. We were probably far away from the camp when she sat me on a log to talk to me.

She said I want you to talk to your people and tell them that the children are mine now. They are being well taken care of and are all healthy. If anyone ever comes looking for them again, the same thing will happen to them as what happened to the man and his dogs.

George said he was told to go now and tell his people. He said as soon as she flew away, he felt that he finally regained control of his body. Everyone in the church was looking in disbelief at George, not quite believing what they were hearing. Now we had an idea of why Constable Shelley and his dogs had no chance to fight back. We also had an idea of the powers that we were dealing with.

Chapter 10
The Plan

Now that we knew for sure that the children were alive and safe, we had to come up with a plan to help our children. However, this plan was already being used somewhat, mostly by the parents of the missing children. Now, the whole community would pitch in and help these parents and children.

It was decided that anyone who wanted to help could pack leftovers in plastic bags and leave them in their back porch cupboards. To make it even easier for the witch to ascertain that there was food available for them, everyone who left food out was asked to leave a white towel somewhere on their back porch; it wouldn't take the witch very long to figure out what this indicated.

This same system was used for anyone who wanted to leave any clothing out for the children. Over the space of a few weeks, it was plain to see that this system was working very well; the food and clothing that was being left out were being picked up on a regular basis. If nothing else, it gave the parents peace of mind knowing that their children were being cared for.

However, we had to let the witch know that we did not want to lose any more children. A security system of sorts was set up; patrols were set up from dusk till daylight every night. Two groups of three men in each group patrolled every night. Two crude shelters were built on each end of the village. These shelters were basic, with only a roof with no walls. This shelter afforded the men shelter from the rain, where they could have coffee and snacks. A fire next to this shelter would be going all night for warmth and light. The men were all armed with rifles, although it was only for show. They had all been instructed that no matter what happened, they were not to fire at the witch. This show of arms and security was hopefully to discourage the witch from leaving our children alone. As we would find out, it did not deter her at all!!

In the weeks that followed, the witch was sighted many times, coming and going from our village. Another winter was pretty much over, and temperatures were increasingly much better every day. Until the day we could get our children back, the plan we had instigated would remain in place.

Chapter 11
Karen & William

With the weather getting warmer every day, my children were eagerly waiting for the day when they could go swimming again. Karen was now fourteen, and William was twelve. Thankfully, they had finally gotten over the loss of their mother and didn't have that perpetual sad look that they once had. I was happy with what I saw in my children; they were both very responsible and extremely respectful children. They both realized that without their mother, the responsibilities for us all had changed. I no longer had to keep after them both to make sure that they did their share of chores. The one thing I felt sorry for was that children this young should not have the burden of so many responsibilities.

Karen did some cooking; I did the cooking for the most part. Karen also did most of the housework and laundry duties, as did I. My routine was the same every year; as soon as most of the snow was gone, I would go into the forest behind our village to fall trees and buck it up. I would use a wheelbarrow to haul it to our house. In two weeks, I had quite a pile in front of our wood shed. It was Williams' chore to pack all the split wood into the woodshed and pile it…but, as usual, his sister would always pitch in packing and piling it.

I never did have to ask them to do this, and once in a while, they would even swap jobs.

The day Karen went missing was such a day; She was doing Williams's chore by filling our woodshed. That day was a sunny, warm day. At dinner time that day, I asked William to call Karen in for dinner. A few minutes later, Willaim came in and said, 'Dad, she's not there, and it looks like she didn't do much!?' Alarmed, I ran outside to see what might have happened. I could see the sweater that she had been using sitting on a block of wood, and the door was left open. I know she was too responsible to leave without letting me know first. I did the only thing I could think of: I ran to the church with my rifle. When I got there, I fired three shots toward the ocean, knowing there was no chance of injuring anyone; within about ten minutes, almost everyone in the village had responded to my shots of distress. I explained what happened and asked if anyone had seen her, and no one had. I knew deep down that this had to be the work of the Witch. It was brazen of her to do something like this in broad daylight. I also knew that it was hopeless to mount searches. This land had been totally scoured by the best trackers and hunters on this land. I announced myself to the People of my decision.

Needless to say, William and I had no appetite for dinner that day; we were both absolutely crushed. William, I would have to say, was stronger Physically and mentally than most twelve-year-olds. This was because of the loss of his mom, which increased his mental toughness. I myself had started helping my father and grandfather with the firewood at the age of ten and had started William helping me at that age also.

While having breakfast the next morning, I could see that William seemed to be deep in thought, so I finally asked him if he was okay. He said, 'Dad, let the Witch take me.' I said, 'Absolutely NOT! I will not let my last child be taken!' He replied, 'If she takes me, I will be able to let Uhbadee know where they are. I could see the logic in what he was saying, but. I DID NOT want to lose both my children. The next few days were very tough on William and me; the house felt empty without Karen being there.'

Until we found a way to bring the children home, life had to go on as normal as possible. Our whole family had a routine; we took turns sending dinner up for UhBadee as he found it too difficult to cook for himself. This day was my turn to do that, and when it was ready, William left to bring a plate of dinner up to UhBaDee.

An hour after William left to bring him his dinner and still hadn't returned, I immediately jogged up to UhBaDees' house to the devastating news that William had not arrived there. I did not have to go home to get my rifle for the distress signal; UhBaDee still had a couple of rifles from his much younger days. After I had explained to the people what happened and told them of my decision to again suspend any plans of a search party, I did this with a very heavy heart, knowing that it was fruitless to even attempt searching. The Witch was too smart; she never left any clues as to where they/He were. Might be.

I went home to a dinner that would remain uneaten. Now, I was beyond being crushed.

The next couple of days, it was as if I was in a fog, with no desire to do anything at all.

I think that long ago, I came to the realization that there was no one to help us. Somehow, we had to find a way to rid ourselves of our huge problem and get our children back.

Chapter 12
Homeward Bound

Two days after William had been taken, UhBaDee sent for me, and I know every time he had sent for me, it was for something important.

I arrived at Uhbadee's house, and he said pour yourself some coffee, Son; we have some planning to do. Right away, I could see that whatever he had to talk about was very serious. As I sat down, he said I have been talking to William. He knows where they are now, and he said we already know how to get there. They are at the back end of that high mountain that is northeast of here. I knew which mountain he meant. This mountain had no name yet, and the only way I can describe it was majestic looking. This is the mountain we had seen with mist coming from the back of it on a clear day.

We had seen this during one of our searches.

UhBaDee said we have to make arrangements as soon as possible, and we should leave no later than two days from now. I said, UhBaDee, what do you mean by 'We? you don't think you can come with us, do you?' He said, 'You can't overcome this Witch without my help, Son.' I said, 'UhBaDee, it will take a whole day for the healthy men just to get to this mountain!' He said, 'Believe me, Son, I know I will make it, and you will definitely need me there.'

UhBaDee said we had no time now but that he would explain how we were to overcome the Witch. He already knew that firearms were useless against her. I knew already of UhBaDees and Williams's telepathic powers and didn't know what other powers he might possess. He said, 'Wait a minute, I'll be right back.' He went into the kitchen and came back with a two-and-a-half-foot machete. He said, 'Work on this until it is razor sharp, and you must make it very sharp.' I said, 'Is this for the Witch, and if it is, how do you expect me to get close enough to her to use it!?' He replied, 'You leave that to me; I will explain later.'

UhBaDee said, 'Now take my rifle to signal the people and tell them we will leave in two days.' he said we would leave it to the people to select six of our strongest men to accompany us, and they must bring enough food for ten and the children. Within half an hour after my signal, most of the people had assembled in the church. I made the announcement of where the children were and what the plans were. The whole church was buzzing, with everyone talking at once. The excitement was almost palpable.

I also let everyone know that it was up to them to pick the six men for this rescue trip. I told them we would leave at daybreak in two days.

Two days later, we were all gathered outside the church: myself, UhBaDee, and the six men the community had picked to accompany us. It was no surprise to me that they had included my brother, as he was one of the Haisla's best hunters and out doorman. The minister had all eight of us join hands with him as he said a prayer for us.

No matter which way you looked at it, this was going to be a very difficult trip for us all. UhBaDee had finally told me that he had the power to control the Witch, for what he said was only for a few seconds in order for me to get the job done. He explained that his theory was that the only way to kill this Witch was to behead her. His reasoning was that the Witch knew this and thought this was the only way to kill anyone, which is why she had beheaded the constable and his dogs.

All six of the men took turns helping UhBaDee on this arduous journey. We tried to pick the least difficult route possible. UhBaDee was a very proud man, and he pushed himself as hard as he could in order not to slow us down. I kept a close eye on him, and when I could see he needed to rest, I would make it seem like we all needed to rest. We made fairly good progress and made camp that first day as darkness neared.

We had decided before leaving our village that there would be no campfires, which might alert the Witch of our presence. Whatever food we had brought was precooked, and we had only water.

On our second day, we made it to the base of the mountain fairly late in the day. We were close, so close we had to be as quiet as possible. We made camp, and after we had our cold food and water, we sat in a tight circle and discussed our plans. Since UhBaDee's eyesight was very poor, he said, 'Do you see a small standing alder?' I said, 'It's not too far from where we are.' He replied, 'William said behind those alders is where the trail starts up the mountain. It was decided that in order to avoid detection, only UhBaDee and I would go up the mountain; the rest of the men would stay put here until they heard our firearms signal.'

At this time of year, it would be bright enough at 04:00 a.m. for myself and UhBaDee to start up the mountain. I would tie a rope around my chest with a loop in the back; this was so UhBaDee could put one hand through the loop and hand onto me for our journey up the mountain. The trail on the side of this mountain, which I thought must be an animal trail of some kind, was between eighteen and twenty-four inches wide.

As I said earlier, UhBaDee wouldn't tell me when he needed to rest, so I made sure to pay attention to the sound of his breathing. When his breathing would get faster, I would tell him that I needed to rest. On one of our rest stops, UhBaDee said that William had told him that there was a small tree growing out from the side of the mountain, pointed out at about ninety degrees from the mountain. He said that tree was approximately about two hundred feet from the cave they were held in. He also said when we get close, we will see the mist emanating from this cave.

We had been traveling up this mountain now for about three and a half hours when we finally reached this small tree that William had mentioned. I told UhBaDee, and he motioned for me to sit down. He said, 'Son, you will have only one chance at this, so your aim must be true. This Witch has so much power, and I hope I can hold her long enough for you to do your job.' As he said all this, he hugged me and said, 'Pray for us, Son.' We were minutes away now, so UhBaDee removed the rope, 'it might slow you down; I will hand onto your jacket.'

This was the moment of truth as we were very close to the entrance of the cave.

The sun was fairly high in the sky now and afforded us good light into the cave. UhBaDee pulled me back and indicated to me that now he would take the lead. I put my hand on his right shoulder as we entered the cave. I immediately felt UhBaDees's whole body go taut. He stood stock still and stared at the Witch, who was standing in front of a crude shack. The Witch was shaking and appeared as if she was trying to break out of a huge vise. I didn't need any prompting; as I ran towards her, I was also drawing back the machete, preparing for the strike at her neck. Thankfully, my aim was true, and the machete was so sharp that I felt no resistance whatsoever. I spun around and looked at a grotesque sight. The Witches mouth was wide open in a silent scream with eyes that were bulging. There was no time for a feeling of triumph as I saw UhBaDee lying on his back! I ran to him to see that his breathing was labored. He said, 'We don't know for sure if her power is gone! So Take her head and throw it off the cliff as far as you can!' I did this and immediately returned to UhBaDee; he said, 'Take me out into the sunlight, Son.' I did as he asked, and he said hold me, Son, my time has come. I held his head in my lap as he continued to try to speak. I could no longer understand what he was trying to say. I held him in my arms with tears streaming down my face until I heard him draw his last breath.

I instructed the children to go back into the cave and take whatever they needed and told them we needed at least two or three blankets. I told them that I would be back in a few minutes. I went back to the small tree where I had left my rifle.

When I got there, I fired off three shots at the six men at the bottom of the mountain.

When I got back to see that the children had done as instructed, I could also see that there had been a rock slide about a hundred feet close to the cave. I asked the children to help carry rocks back to the cave. I said to them, pick the ones light enough for you to carry. When we had enough, I was so sorry that the children had to see this, but I couldn't do this without their help. We carried the rocks into the cave and piled them onto the witch's body.

It was at this time that I saw what the witch had done, and it was ingenious. She had used free sapling for the framework of the crude shack that she had built. The shack was built to keep the moisture out. This heat probably came from hot springs from within the mountain. This is how they survived the harsh winters.

Now, we were ready to start our journey down the mountain. I instructed the children to stay as far away from the outer edge of the trail as possible and that we must not rush. As with most elderly people, UhBaDee had lost a lot of weight; I carried him out in what is termed a firearms carry. He only weighed about ninety pounds. The six Haislas were very fast, and we were only about a quarter way down when they met us.

When we got to the bottom, we stopped and made plans; there were about three hours of daylight, and we would push on as fast as we could. We expected that the trip home would be faster than our tip here because now, without UhBaDee's slower pace walk and the men taking turns carrying him, the pace homeward bound would be much faster.

We thought that the best plan would be to cut two poles for a makeshift stretcher, which we did. We strung rope back and forth between the two poles to make this stretcher and used three of the children's blankets. Now we were ready, we covered UhBaDee with one of the blankets and secured him with rope also. As we got underway, I thought of the events of this day. I thought that the strain of the trip to get here and the trip up the mountain contributed to UhBaDee's demise.

I also was thinking that if it was only the hard journey that he had to deal with, it would not have caused his demise. I think that it was the tremendous strain of controlling the witch with his mind that proved to be too much for this old body.

In the three hours of daylight that we had left, we had covered a great amount of distance. The children were so excited to be going home that they needed no prodding to move fast.

The next morning, after having a cold cooked moose meat and water, we were underway at approximately four thirty, a very early start. By about three in the afternoon, we knew that we could make it home that day.

At five in the afternoon, we were about four miles from our village. I instructed one of the men to fire two shots into the air. I need not have worried about our people not hearing this. The whole community had been waiting for this signal.

As we entered our village, it was a scene that we will never forget: the children running for their families. I don't think there was a dry eye in the whole community.

Tears of joy as we didn't think we would ever see our children again. As for myself, I felt D??? to the task of getting UhBaDee home.

I felt that I had neglected my children after the initial hugs and also a few tears; I had been too busy attending to all the tasks of getting everyone home.

With all this joy happening, the only thing I felt was great sadness. Thankfully, the six men who accompanied us stuck by my side. I instructed most of the men to find a tarp and meet us at the church. We carried UhBaDee into the church, which is where he would stay until the funeral tomorrow. When the tarp arrived, we carefully wrapped UhBaDee in it and wrapped rope around it quite tightly; this is how he would be put into a cedar box, which would be constructed very quickly.

That night, there would be two shifts of four men in each crew that would sit with UhBaDee through the night.

UhBaDee was a very pragmatic man and had long since cleared what he chose as his final resting place decades beforehand. As there was probably only two and a half of soil, there he had packed enough rock to cover his grave. To many, this may have seemed a bit morbid, but UhBaDee did not want to trouble anyone.

Chapter 13
The Final Goodbye

Throughout the night, our local carpenter had constructed a Red Cedar casket for UhBaDee. In this day and age, when someone passes away, things have to be done very quickly. At ten o'clock the next morning, everyone gathered at the church for a short service. I had written a short eulogy for UhBaDee.

As I read the eulogy, I also mentioned what everyone already knew, that UhBaDee had given his life to bring their children home. As I was reading this part, everyone showed their respect by all standing and remained standing until I had finished reading the eulogy.

As the service came to an end, the casket was carried out of the church, and we started the walk to the grave site.

We were accompanied by our song and dance group, and this is something that will always be ingrained in my memory. The drums that were used were the larger drums with a much deeper tone. They sang what was called "The Mourning Song". The men would sing one verse in their deeper voices, and the women would sing an answering verse in their higher voices, accompanied by deep-sounding drums… Boom! Boom! Boom! This sound never failed to cause me to have good bumps.

It took about twenty minutes to reach the grave site. When we arrived there, I observed that some of the men had already prepared the grave site. They had dug down only about two feet before hitting the rock.

The casket was put into this hole that had been dug, and then all the rock that had been gathered was piled on top of what little soil there was.

When all this had been done, our minister conducted a short prayer service.

When the minister was done, I stood beside UhBaDee's grave site and thanked all The People for all of their help and for allowing myself and my children some privacy.

When everyone had left, I held the hands of my two children and spoke to UhBaDee as if he could hear me, and he probably could. I thanked him for sacrificing his life to bring The Children home. As we stood there, I finally understood why he had picked this spot for his final resting place. From this point, we could see part of our village, and on this calm sunny day, we could see the sun glistening off The Douglas Channel. In life, UhBaDee had lost most of his vision. Where he is now, he has full vision and will always be seeing the land that he loved so much and The People he loved so much (*even more?).